Kim

The Extraordinary Adventures of an Ordinary Hat

Wolfram Hänel

The Extraordinary Adventures of an Ordinary Hat

PICTURES BY

Christa Unzner-Fischer

TRANSLATED BY

J. Alison James

North-South Books

NEW YORK

Copyright © 1994 by Nord-Süd Verlag AG, Gossau Zürich, Switzerland
First published in Switzerland under the title *Waldemar und die weite Welt*
English translation copyright © 1994 by North-South Books Inc.

First published in the United States, Great Britain, Canada,
Australia, and New Zealand in 1994 by North-South Books,
an imprint of Nord-Süd Verlag AG, Gossau Zürich, Switzerland.

Distributed in the United States by North-South Books Inc., New York.

Library of Congress Cataloging-in-Publication Data is available.
ISBN 1-55858-255-X (TRADE BINDING)
ISBN 1-55858-256-8 (LIBRARY BINDING)

A CIP catalogue record for this book
is available from The British Library.

1 3 5 7 9 10 8 6 4 2
Printed in Belgium

He was not unusual in any way—just an
ordinary black bowler hat. Not too big and
not too small. Not too round and certainly
not pointy. He was really quite normal. Still,
no one wanted to buy him. He had been
around a while. Perhaps he had gone a little
out of fashion.

His place was high on the top shelf, in an out-of-the-way corner. Jonathan, the hat-shop owner, had grown quite fond of him. About once a year, he'd take the hat down and say, "What ever shall I do with you?" Lovingly he would brush off the dust, fluff up the felt, and set the hat back up on the shelf.

The hat really didn't mind being in his corner. At least it was quiet, and he was able to dream to his heart's content.

He daydreamed about faraway lands, and a sweet straw hat with a bright flowing scarf.

Occasionally the hat would be filled with
a desire to belong to someone, so he could
have adventures and see the great wide
world.

When this happened he would tell the
other hats stories of when he was new,
sitting proudly in the shop window. He
could see everything on the entire street.

Back then, things were quite different.

Great old trees lined the street, and the children played a game with spinning tops and string. The bus was pulled by real horses. Only the manager of the bank had a motorcar.

One day, the bank manager came into the hat shop. He decided to buy the hat's twin

brother! Every morning, as he sat in the shop window, the hat watched his brother go from the motorcar to the bank, perched proudly on the head of the bank manager. And every evening he saw them come out of the bank and get back into the car.

"Ah, yes," sighed the hat. "Those were the days. . . ." Then he closed his eyes and began to dream again—of horse-drawn buses, bank managers, and sweet straw hats!

One day a little round man came into the shop.

"Ah, Mr. Bruno," said Jonathan, bowing politely. "How may I help you?"

"A hat," Bruno replied. "I need a hat."

"Of course," said Jonathan. "You've come to the right place!" Eagerly he set out his finest and most expensive hats.

But Bruno pointed up to the topmost shelf. "That bowler," he said. "The one in the corner. That is the hat I want."

"The . . . the bowler?" Jonathan stuttered.
"Of course, how foolish of me," he said
quickly, trying to hide his surprise. "An
excellent choice. They never go out of
style." Tenderly he blew a few stray threads
from the hat's brim.

Before he knew it, the hat was perched like a king on top of Bruno's shining bald head.

Jonathan was so sad at the thought of suddenly losing his longtime friend that tears came to his eyes.

The hat was sad too, and he began to sniffle.

Suddenly, the hat was out in the street. As the door banged shut behind him, he heard the little bell ring for the last time.

The hat clung tightly to Bruno's bald head as he walked down the street. Younger hats might have found this difficult, but the bowler was from the old school. Strong. Dependable. Made to last a lifetime.

Soon they entered a huge, dark room with lots of chairs and a curtain at the front. It was a theatre. They were going to see a movie! Finally, the adventure the hat had been longing for! How wonderful it was to belong to someone!

The curtain parted, and on the screen, a funny man stumbled around. On his head he wore a bowler that was the spitting image of Bruno's hat. The people laughed and hooted and cheered. The hat had never been so proud of being a bowler.

Suddenly the man sitting behind Bruno leaned forward and whispered angrily, "Kindly remove your hat, sir! I cannot see a thing!"

"Oh, forgive me," Bruno stammered. "I didn't know it was in the way." Quickly Bruno pulled the hat off and set it in his lap.

The hat was crushed. He'd wanted so much to see the end of the film. But now he couldn't see a thing.

When the movie was finally over, they came out into the fresh air. What a relief it was to be up on Bruno's bald head again!

Bruno headed straight home. He was late for supper and his wife was not happy.

"Where have you been?" she asked. "And take that ridiculous thing off your head!"

So the hat was cast in the wardrobe, where it was pitch black and smelled wretchedly of mothballs.

Early the next morning Bruno brought him out again. They were going to the office. The hat was looking forward to a day of seeing new things. But before he reached his office, Bruno exchanged the hat for a handsome hairpiece, and the hat spent the rest of the day in a filing cabinet among dusty order forms from the year before last.

And that is the way it was, day in and day out. Every morning he came out of the wardrobe and went into the filing cabinet. Every evening the trip was reversed. Out and in, in and out.

It would have been bearable if at least the walk to the office had been a little fun. But no, Bruno was so short that the hat was jostled and poked by every elbow, umbrella and briefcase that came by!

How he missed his old out-of-the-way place high on the topmost shelf in the corner of the hat shop. He thought longingly of Jonathan.

Then summer came, and with it came the holidays.

One day Bruno and his wife decided to go camping. Bruno took along his bowler to protect him from the sun. The hat was tied on top of the luggage on the roof of the car. There he bounced around in the hot sun until he was quite carsick.

At the campsite Bruno had his hands full
setting up the tent.

The hat lay unnoticed in the high grass.

A rabbit came up to him, waggled his ears,
and said:

"Listen here, old fellow. Could you just
flip yourself over so I could have a
comfortable place to rest?"

So the hat turned himself upside down.
And the rabbit curled up inside him and
sighed in satisfaction.

The two became close friends. They
stayed up late that night, telling each other
long stories and dancing in the light of the
moon.

For the first time in a very long while, the
hat was happy.

When Bruno crawled out of his tent the next morning, he couldn't believe his eyes. A wild rabbit was in his hat, probably filling it with fleas! The rabbit hopped away quickly. And when Bruno went to put his hat on his bald head, an egg fell out! A snow white Easter egg!

Bruno was annoyed. "An Easter egg in summer?" he grumbled, as he carefully inspected the hat. "That is going too far!"

Bruno plucked a couple of rabbit hairs from the brim. "Just you wait!" he threatened. "As soon as we get back home, you're going straight to the cleaners!"

The hat shuddered. He had heard the most terrible things about cleaners. Once one of the other hats in Bruno's wardrobe had gone to the cleaners. When he came back, he was steamed and ironed and pressed —his comfortable old shape was completely gone.

No, the hat could never let that happen to him!

He had to find a way to escape. The very next day he had his chance.

Bruno took him for a walk on the beach.

Over the sea, from strange faraway places, the wind carried the scent of mysterious things.

Escaping was easy. The hat simply
loosened his grip on Bruno's head, and—
wheee!—the wind carried him up and away.

The hat whirled and whistled and swirled, and soon Bruno was only a comical figure with outstretched arms down below on the beach.

Then Bruno was gone, and the hat sailed out over the open water, dreaming of all the wide world he would see, and of the sweet straw hat with the bright flowing scarf. He knew in his heart that someday he would find her.

One morning, many weeks later, a thick
letter arrived for Jonathan. It had a bunch of
jumbled stamps and at least twenty different
postmarks. Curious, he opened the envelope
at once and took out a sheet of paper
covered with tidy handwriting.

It was a very long letter:

My dear Jonathan,

You will be surprised to hear from me in this unusual way. But not as surprised as when you hear that I am no longer with bald old Bruno. I am in South America, where everything is quite different.

Here, chickens are allowed to ride in the buses, and the people are called "muchachos." They speak Spanish, and I am already getting quite good at understanding it. Si, señor.

I belong to a man named Don Leonardo.

We live on a "hacienda" (a farm) with many
"burros" (donkeys). Every day we walk around
the pasture from morning to evening. In the
middle of the day the sun is very hot, so we take
a "siesta" (a rest) in a hammock under the
trees.

And now hold on to your hat: Last week we
got married.

Actually, only Don Leonardo got married, to a beautiful woman named Doña Emilia. But I was there. There was a party, and what a party it was!

(By the way, Doña Emilia is the one writing this letter to you. As you can imagine, my penmanship is not particularly good.)

And you will never guess what else: Doña Emilia wore a hat to her wedding.

Yes, my friend, a hat.

And as if it were destiny, it was a straw hat—a sweet straw hat with a bright flowing scarf!

Now we are together forever, my little straw hat and I.

In the night, we lie under a great mosquito net, next to each other on the windowsill, and dream.

I think of you often and hope that you find as much happiness as I have.

Your friend,

The hat

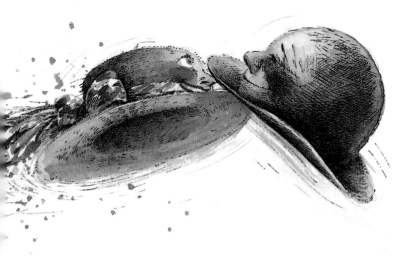

For a long time Jonathan sat at his counter.

He read the hat's letter again and again, until the lines swam before his eyes.

Then without really noticing that it was happening, he began to dream . . . of a distant land filled with donkeys and sweet straw hats.

Christa Unzner-Fischer was born in a small town near Berlin, in what was then part of East Germany. She wanted to become a ballet dancer, but she ended up studying commercial art and working in an advertising agency. She entered a book illustration contest and won third prize, which led to a career as a free-lance illustrator, primarily of children's books. She loves fairy tales and fantasy stories, especially books like *Alice's Adventures in Wonderland.* Christa Unzner-Fischer is married and lives in Berlin.

About the Author

Wolfram Hänel has lived for most of his life in Hannover, Germany. He studied German and English literature and has worked as a photographer, a graphic artist, a copy writer, a teacher, and a playwright. Today Wolfram Hänel writes children's books, plays, and travel guides. He has a wife and a daughter, and would like to live by the sea, or better yet, on an island. There is a little one named Inishturk that would be perfect. It has eighty-four inhabitants, four fishing boats, no cars, and only one telephone . . . .

ABOUT THE TRANSLATOR

J. Alison James was born in southern California but has had many adventures in northern Germany. She studied German and Swedish so she would be able to translate the extraordinary children's books published in those languages. She believes that in books children can discover how similar people are all over the world.

OTHER NORTH-SOUTH EASY-TO-READ BOOKS

Rinaldo, the Sly Fox
by Ursel Scheffler
illustrated by Iskender Gider

•

The Return of Rinaldo, the Sly Fox
by Ursel Scheffler
illustrated by Iskender Gider

•

Loretta and the Little Fairy
by Gerda Marie Scheidl
illustrated by Christa Unzner-Fischer

•

Little Polar Bear and the Brave Little Hare
by Hans de Beer

•

Where's Molly?
by Uli Waas